**Max & Ruby**

**THIS BOOK BELONGS TO:**

_____

# Max and Ruby's Storybook Collection

Max &
Ruby

Max & Ruby © Rosemary Wells and
Series © 2002–2003 Nelvana Limited
Used under licence by Key Porter Books Limited
NELVANA is a registered trademark of Nelvana Limited.
CORUS is a trademark of Corus Entertainment Inc.
All rights reserved.

Library and Archives Canada Cataloguing in Publication

Wells, Rosemary
    Max and Ruby's Storybook Collection/Rosemary Wells,
originating author and illustrator; Harry Endrulat, text
adaptation; illustrations taken from the animated series
Max & Ruby and adapted by Muse Publishing and
Communications Inc.

Includes six stories, previously published separately under
titles: Ruby Riding Hood, Max and the Beanstalk, Ruby's Magic
Act, Max's Birthday, Ruby's Skating Day and Max's Rocket Run.

ISBN 978-1-55470-107-0

    1. Children's stories.  I. Endrulat, Harry  II. Title.

PZ7.W46483Mars 2008     j813'.54     C2007-907652

The publisher gratefully acknowledges the support of the
Canada Council for the Arts and the Ontario Arts Council
for its publishing program. We acknowledge the support
of the Government of Ontario through the Ontario Media
Development Corporation's Ontario Book Initiative.

We acknowledge the financial support of the Government of
Canada through the Book Publishing Industry Development
Program (BPIDP) for our publishing activities.

KPk is an imprint of Key Porter Books Limited
Six Adelaide Street East, Tenth Floor
Toronto, Ontario
Canada  M5C 1H6

www.keyporter.com

Book adaptation by
Muse Publishing and Communications Inc.
www.musecommunications.ca

Text adaptation by Harry Endrulat

Printed and bound in China
08 09 10 11 12 6 5 4 3 2 1

# Table of Contents

# Ruby Riding Hood

Once upon a time, there was a little bunny named Ruby.
She wore a red hood so everyone called her Ruby Riding Hood.
One day, Ruby Riding Hood decided to take Grandma a basket of cookies.

On the way to Grandma's house, she met the Big Max Wolf.
He was very hungry. He reached for the basket.
"Cookies!" said the Big Max Wolf.

Just as he was about to grab the basket, Ruby Riding Hood pulled it away.
"I'm sorry," said Ruby Riding Hood. "These cookies are for Grandma."
And away she went.

Ruby Riding Hood walked through the forest.
After a while, she got tired and decided to rest by a tree.

Ruby Riding Hood didn't realize that
the Big Max Wolf had followed her.

The Big Max Wolf reached toward the basket.
"Cookies!" said the Big Max Wolf.

Just as he was about to grab the basket, Ruby Riding Hood pulled it away.
"I'm sorry," said Ruby Riding Hood. "These cookies are for Grandma."
And away she went.

Ruby Riding Hood stopped at the playground.
She put the basket at the bottom of the slide
and played on the swing.

Ruby Riding Hood didn't realize that the
Big Max Wolf had followed her again.

The Big Max Wolf climbed to the top of the slide.
He slid down and reached toward the basket.
"Cookies!" said the Big Max Wolf.

Just as he was about to grab the basket, Ruby Riding Hood pulled it away.
"I'm sorry," said Ruby Riding Hood. "These cookies are for Grandma."
And away she went.

The Big Max Wolf watched Ruby Riding Hood skip away.
He was very hungry, but he did not know how to get the cookies.

Then the Big Max Wolf had an idea.
While Ruby Riding Hood talked to the woodcutter…

15

…the Big Max Wolf took a shortcut to Grandma's house!

He put on Grandma's shawl and waited in the kitchen.

Ruby Riding Hood arrived at Grandma's house.
"Hi, Grandma. Would you like to try some
of the cookies I made?" she asked.

Grandma reached toward the basket.
"Grandma, what funny-looking ears you have!"
said Ruby Riding Hood.

Grandma grabbed the basket.
"Grandma, what dusty little hands you have!"
said Ruby Riding Hood.

"Cookies!" said the Big Max Wolf.

Just then, the real Grandma walked into the room.
The Big Max Wolf hid behind the shawl.
"Hi, Ruby. You brought me cookies!" said Grandma.

Ruby Riding Hood looked at Grandma.
Ruby Riding Hood looked at the other Grandma.
"But how can there be two Grandmas?" she asked.

23

The Big Max Wolf threw off the shawl.
"Max! Or should I say the Big Max Wolf!"
laughed Ruby Riding Hood.

Grandma looked in the basket.
"Well, there's plenty for everyone.
We can all have some delicious…"

"Cookies!" said the Big Max Wolf.

# Max and the Beanstalk

Once upon a time, there was a little bunny named Max.
He lived with his big sister, Ruby.

One day, Ruby was very hungry.
She gave Max three coins.
"Take these coins to the market and get us something to eat," she said.

Max took the three coins.
He grabbed his red rubber elephant and left the house.

At the market, there were many yummy fruits and vegetables.
*Max didn't know which to choose!*

"Hello there, Max," said Mr. Piazza.
"Are you looking for something good?"
Max nodded his head yes.

"I've got just the thing," said Mr. Piazza.
He opened his hand.

"Beans," said Mr. Piazza.
Max didn't like beans.

"But not ordinary beans," said Mr. Piazza.
"These beans are magic!"

Max didn't like beans, but he loved magic.
He took out his three coins to pay for the beans.

"Well, Max, I'll let you have these magic beans," said Mr. Piazza.
"But it'll cost you those three coins – and your red rubber elephant."

"Beans!" said Max.
Max paid Mr. Piazza, took the beans and left the store.

When Max got home, Ruby was waiting for him.
"I'm so glad you're back, Max," she said.
"What did you get from the market?"

Max opened his hands.
"Beans!" said Max.

"You spent our money and traded your red rubber elephant
for three little beans?" asked Ruby.

Ruby took the beans from Max.
She walked outside.
Max followed.

"Magic," said Max.
"I think you've been tricked, Max," said Ruby.
"There's no such thing as magic beans."

Ruby threw the beans on the ground.
"Beans," said Max.
But Ruby took Max back into the house.

That night, while Max and Ruby slept, the beans started to grow.
And grow and grow and grow.

They grew into a giant beanstalk!

The next morning, Max woke up early and went outside.
He saw the giant beanstalk.
"Beans!" said Max.

50

Max started to climb the beanstalk.
He climbed and climbed and climbed until he reached the top.

In the clouds he found baskets of fruit and vegetables.
He found baskets of his favourite candies.
And he found a brand-new red rubber elephant.

Max picked up a basket of food and the red rubber elephant.
He climbed back down the beanstalk.
Ruby stood at the bottom waiting for him.

53

"I can't believe you found all this food!" Ruby said.
"I guess they really were magic…"
"Beans!" said Max.

Ruby and Louise were practising their magic act
for the Bunny Scouts Talent Show.
But they needed a volunteer.

Ruby and Louise had the same idea. "Max!"

Of course, Max was happy to volunteer.

For the first magic trick, Ruby pulled a coin from Max's ear.

"How?" asked Max.
"A great magician never tells how a trick is done," said Ruby.

For the second magic trick, Louise poured a pitcher full of milk
into a rolled-up newspaper cone. Not one drop of milk dripped out.

Max peeked inside the newspaper cone.
The milk had magically disappeared!

Next, Ruby pulled a yellow handkerchief from her sleeve…
and a blue one…and a green one…and a purple one…
and a red one…and an orange one – with flowers at the end!

"How?" asked Max.
"Magic," whispered Ruby.

Ruby and Louise got ready for the Great Disappearing Trick.
They did not see Max sneak away.

Max found a secret door at the back of the Magic Box.
He had an idea for a trick of his own. He stepped into the box.

Ruby and Louise were now ready for the Great Disappearing Trick.
But their volunteer was gone!
"Maybe Max went into the box," said Louise.

Inside the box, Max heard Ruby and Louise.
He did not want to be found.
What could he do?

Max opened the secret door.
He slipped out the back of the Magic Box.

Max hid behind the box as Ruby came to check inside.

Ruby opened the door. The Magic Box was empty.
"Let's look behind it," said Ruby.

When Ruby closed the front door, Max opened the back door.
He climbed inside the Magic Box again.

Ruby and Louise could not find Max. He had disappeared!
"Now we don't have an audience," said Ruby.

"An audience for what?" asked Grandma, entering the yard.
"Our Great Disappearing Trick!" said Ruby.

"Oh, I love disappearing tricks!" said Grandma.
"How exciting!"
Ruby and Louise began the show.

"Now we will perform the Great Disappearing Trick," said Ruby.
"Before your very eyes, I will make Louise disappear from this Magic Box."
But before Louise could step into the box…

79

Max reappeared!

"What a wonderful trick!" said Grandma.

"How?" asked Ruby and Louise.
"Magic!" said Max.

Max & Ruby

# Max's Birthday

It was Max's birthday.
He had a big party with chocolate cake.

He got lots of presents – pajamas from Uncle Frank,
a steam train from the Huffingtons
and three wind-up chicks from his sister, Ruby.

Beside the couch, Ruby found one gift that was still wrapped.
"Max! There's a present you forgot to open!" said Ruby.

Max stopped playing with the little yellow chicks.
He rushed over to see.

Ruby read the card.
"Happy Birthday, Max. From Aunt Claire and Uncle Nate."
Max couldn't wait to open his present.

"I wonder what it is," said Ruby.
Max was so excited he ripped off all the wrapping paper
and tore open the box.

"It's a wind-up lobster. Say hello, Max," said Ruby.
Max didn't want to say hello. He was afraid of the lobster.
"No," he said.

The lobster climbed out of the box.
"It wants to play tag," said Ruby.
"No," said Max.

Max ran into the kitchen.
The lobster still wanted to play. It followed Max.

In the kitchen, Max played with his little yellow chicks.
He laughed as they splashed in the water.

The lobster wanted to play too.
"No," said Max.
The lobster would not stop. It knocked over the bowl.

Max had an idea. He ran outside.

The lobster still wanted to play. It followed Max.

Max ran back inside the house.
He closed the door and hid.

Ruby found Max hiding under the dining room table.
He had the last piece of chocolate birthday cake.

The lobster found Max there too.
Before Max could take one bite of the cake,
the lobster took it away.

"No," said Max.
The lobster would not stop. It crashed into the couch.
Cake flew everywhere.

Then the lobster chased Max around the kitchen table…

through the hallway…

and into the living room.

"Watch out for the box, Max!" warned Ruby.
But it was too late.

Max tripped over the box and fell onto his back.
The lobster climbed on top of Max.
Little lobster feet tickled Max's belly.

Ruby grabbed the wind-up toy.
"Let's put the lobster away,
so he won't scare you any more."

"No," said Max.
He took the lobster back from Ruby.
"Again!"

Max & Ruby

# Ruby's Skating Day

Max, Ruby and Louise were going skating.

Ruby and Louise wanted to
practise their figure eights.

Max wanted to skate with the big bunnies.
"Hockey!" said Max.

"You can't play hockey yet, Max," said Ruby.
"First you have to learn to skate."
Ruby helped Max put on his skates.
Louise helped Max put on his helmet.

Max walked onto the ice.
He took a couple of steps.
He flapped his arms.
He fell down.

"I think he needs some lessons," said Louise.
"Don't worry, Max," said Ruby.
"I've got something to help you learn to skate."

Ruby gave Max a chair.
Max held onto the chair and started
skating around the rink.

Ruby put on her skates.
She was ready.

Ruby started her figure eight.
Then she spotted Max.
He was skating toward the hockey players!

Ruby hurried over to stop him.
"Hockey!" said Max.

"You can't play hockey yet, Max," said Ruby.
"First you have to learn to skate."

Ruby pushed Max away from the hockey game.
"You practise skating here, Max," said Ruby.
"Louise and I are going to practise our figure eights."

Ruby started her figure eight.
Then she spotted Max.
He was skating toward the hockey players again!

Ruby hurried over to stop him.
"Hockey!" said Max.

"You can't play hockey yet, Max," said Ruby.
"First you have to learn to skate. Right, Roger?"
Roger, one of the big bunnies playing hockey, agreed.
"Uh-huh," he said.

Ruby pushed Max away from the hockey game.
"You practise skating here, Max," said Ruby.
"Louise and I are going to practise our figure eights."

As Max sat in his chair, a conga line skated past.
Max grabbed the scarf of the last bunny.

Ruby started her figure eight.
Then she spotted Max.
He was part of the conga line!

As Ruby watched, Max let go of the scarf.
He glided in front of the hockey net!
"Don't worry, Max!" yelled Ruby.
"I'll get you!"

Ruby skated toward Max.
Roger skated toward Ruby.
Ruby turned to miss Roger.

Ruby turned and skated toward Max again.
A group of players skated toward Ruby.
Ruby turned to miss them.

135

Ruby turned and skated toward Max again.
Ruby pushed Max away from the hockey game.
"Ruby! You made a perfect figure eight!" said Louise.

Roger skated up and passed Max the puck.
Max kicked the puck.
The puck slid into the net.

"Max scores!" said Ruby.
"Hockey!" said Max.

# Max's Rocket Run

Max got a new Speed Demon sled for Christmas.

He wanted to ride down Rocket Run.

"Oh no, Max," said Max's older sister, Ruby.
"Rocket Run is for big bunnies," said Louise.

Ruby took Max to Bunny Hill.
She hopped onto the back of his sled.
"One, two, three. Whee!" yelled Ruby.

They went down the hill very slowly.
"Faster," said Max.

They climbed to the top of Bunny Hill.
"This time I'll give you a big push," said Ruby.
"One, two, three. Whee!" yelled Ruby.

Max went down the hill very slowly.
"Faster," said Max.

Max climbed to the top of Bunny Hill.
"This time Louise and I will push you," said Ruby.
"One, two, three. Whee!" yelled Ruby and Louise together.

Max went down the hill very slowly.
"Faster," said Max.
He still wanted to ride down Rocket Run.

"Oh no, Max," said Ruby.
"Rocket Run is for big bunnies," said Louise.

Ruby, Louise and Max walked to Rocket Run.
Big bunnies were going down the hill very fast.

Ruby and Louise were scared.

"Still want to go?" asked Ruby.
"Sure…if you do," said Louise.

"We can do it," said Ruby.
"Of course we can," said Louise.

"Bunny Scouts are brave and true.
When a job must be done, what do we do?
Hop to it!" said Ruby and Louise together.

Ruby and Louise were ready for Rocket Run.
But their toboggan was missing!

Max was missing too!
But his Speed Demon sled was still there.

Ruby and Louise looked down Rocket Run.
Max was racing down the hill on their toboggan!
"Faster!" yelled Max.

Ruby and Louise hopped on Max's Speed Demon sled.
They raced down the hill after Max.

Max hit a big bump.
He flew through the air.

Ruby and Louise hit a big bump.
They flew through the air.

Everyone landed in a big pile of snow.

"Max. Are you all right?" asked Ruby.

"Faster!" yelled Max.

CUT ALONG DOTTED LINES

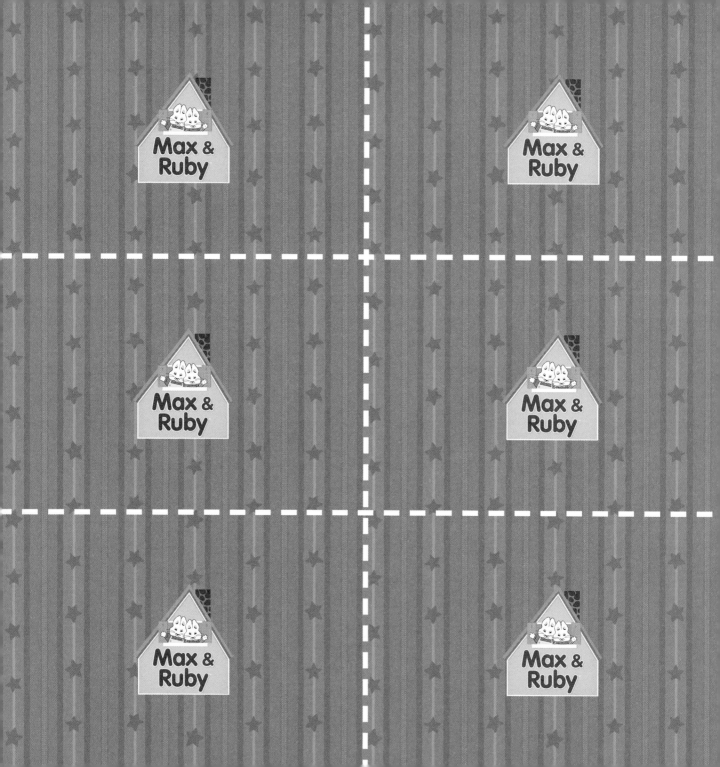

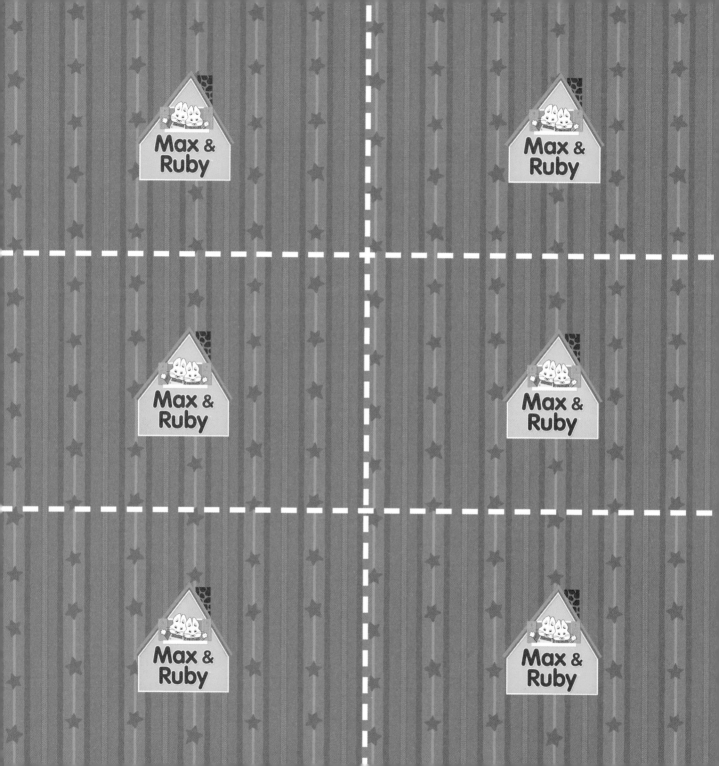

CUT ALONG DOTTED LINES

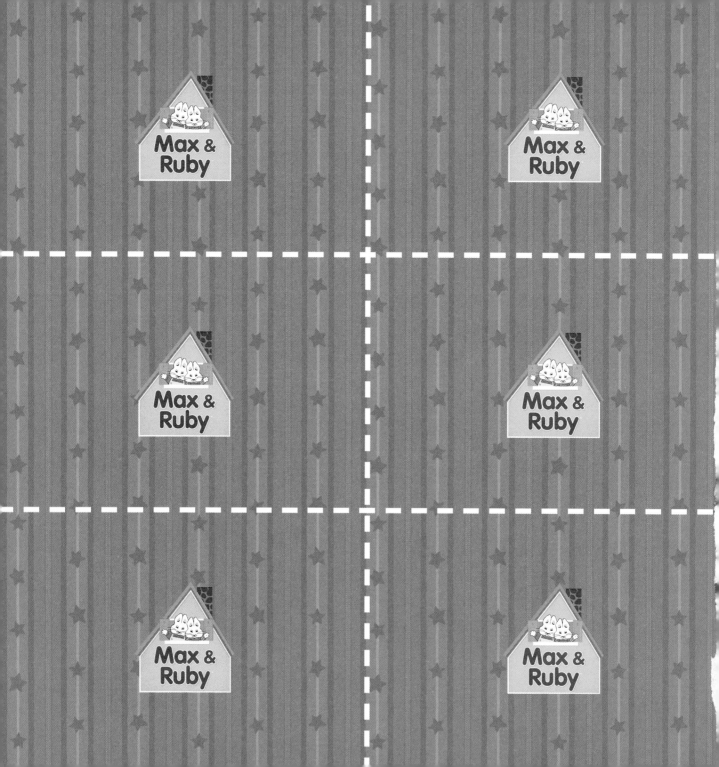